DANGER!
You are on board the Mobius Express when the Star Crystal, the most valuable jewel in the galaxy, is stolen.

YOUR MISSION:
Find out who has stolen the crystal before they can escape the Mobius Express.

Bantam Books in the
Be An Interplanetary Spy Series

BE AN INTERPLANETARY SPY™ 6

THE STAR CRYSTAL

by Ron Martinez

based on a story by
Byron Preiss and Ron Martinez
illustrated by Rich Larson
and Steve Fastner

*A
Byron Preiss
Book*

BANTAM BOOKS
TORONTO · NEW YORK · LONDON · SYDNEY

To my parents, Marie and Moises Martinez.

Ron Martinez is a free-lance writer who lives in Manhattan with his lovely wife, Anne Teshima. His work has appeared in *The Secret Life of Cats* and *Heavy Metal* magazine. He is currently completing a novel entitled *Great Alien Short Stories*.

Steve Fastner and Rich Larson create posters, prints and publication covers for Sal Q. Warren and other purveyors of the fantastic. Their studio is in Minneapolis, Minnesota.

RL3, IL age 9 and up

THE STAR CRYSTAL
A Bantam Book/January 1984

Special thanks to Judy Gitenstein, Laure Smith, Ron Buehl, Anne Greenberg, Lucy Salvino, Lisa Novak, Seth McEvoy, Ann Weil, Evelyn Daley, Len Neufeld and Anne Teshima.

Cover art by Rich Larson and Steve Fastner.

Additional design and production by Rich Larson and Steve Fastner

Cover and series design by Marc Hempel.

"BE AN INTERPLANETARY SPY" is a trademark of Byron Preiss Visual Publications, Inc.

Typesetting by Graphic/Data Services.

Introduction

You are an Interplanetary Spy. You are about to embark on a dangerous mission. On your mission you will face challenges that may result in your death.

You work for the Interplanetary Spy Center, a far-reaching organization devoted to stopping crime and terrorism in the galaxy. While you are on your mission, you will take your orders from the Interplanetary Spy Center. Follow your instructions carefully.

You will be traveling alone on your mission. If you are captured, the Interplanetary Spy Center will not be able to help you. Only your wits and your sharp spy skills will help you reach your goal. Be careful. Keep your eyes open at all times.

If you are ready to meet the challenge of being an Interplanetary Spy, turn to page 1.

You are an Interplanetary Spy,
traveling in a small space pod. You
have just entered the atmosphere
of the planet Teledar, in sector 11.
To receive information about your
mission, enter your Interplanetary
Spy ISBN code number below.

If you are not sure of the code number,
check the back cover of this book.

Turn to page 2.

Your mission is to guard the interplanetary diplomat Quarboss Tro as he travels from Teledar to the headquarters of the Galactic Arts Council on the planet Mirado.

Tro will deliver to the council a unique and priceless jewel known as the Star Crystal. The council will present the Star Crystal to the artist whose work they feel is the greatest in the galaxy.

Interplanetary Spy Center has learned that someone is plotting to steal the Star Crystal. You must make sure that Tro and the Star Crystal get safely to Mirado.

You will be disguised as an art expert from the planet Kron. For this mission you will use the name:

D A R K S T A R

You and Tro will travel to Mirado on the Mobius Express, a new type of spacecraft.

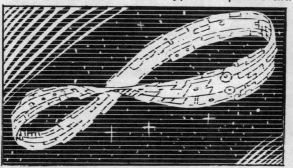

You will meet Tro on the planet Teledar. Another Interplanetary Spy, code name Rolo, will take you to Tro.

Turn to page 9.

You assembled the bioform mask pieces in the wrong order. You'll look very silly wearing this!

You'll have to keep out of sight until an Interplanetary Spy shuttle craft can pick you up. And that won't be for six months!

You run to the right. This corridor opens out into a large, crowded room. The pyramid is a market, patrolled by Teledarian police. That must be why the thieves stayed outside!

You leave the pyramid through a doorway at the far end of the market. You continue through the city.

In a short time you arrive at the maintenance tunnel.

Turn to page 12.

Tro locks the Star Crystal in a carrying case. As you follow him out to the roof of the building, you scan the area for any sign of the attackers.

You and Tro enter a space jumper—a small craft designed to travel through the jump-doors in the Teledarian atmosphere.

Tro inserts a cylinder into the jumper's control panel. "Rolo gave this to me," says Tro. A diagram of your course appears on the screen. Your destination: Grell, a jungle world in sector 12.

Go on to the next page.

The course diagram will determine which of the two jump-doors you will use. The course diagram should be able to fit over the jump-door diagram so that none of the shapes in the two diagrams overlap.

Which jump-door should you use?

This one?
Turn to
page 28.

This one?
Turn to
page 33.

You land your shuttle on platform B. Your shuttle is locked into place, and you begin to move toward the passenger areas.

Soon the shuttle comes to a stop. You look out the window and realize that you're underwater! "This must be the aquatic section," says Tro. "It's where the water passengers stay!"

You landed on the wrong platform. Turn back to page 40 and try again.

You are now well within the atmosphere
of Teledar. You will make a secret landing
on the outskirts of Centar, the capital city.
Fire retro rockets.

Touchdown!

Computer scan shows your landing was undetect-
ed! **Turn to page 10.**

You remove your disguise from a storage compartment in the pod. First, you change into the clothing of a Kronian art expert. Next, you pull on a pair of bioform gloves. The material looks and feels exactly like real skin.

Now you are ready for the bioform mask. The mask is made up of six separate pieces. Starting with the top of the mask, you must join the pieces in the correct order. When the mask is assembled, pull it over your head.

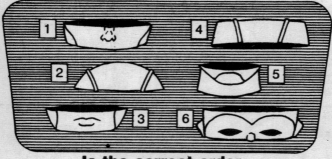

**Is the correct order
2-4-6-1-3-5?
Turn to page 15.**

**Is the correct order
6-2-3-1-4-5?
Turn to page 4.**

You set off to the right. As you walk through the streets of Centar, you spot groups of buildings that you recognize from the map. You're on the right track.

You see a group of Teledarians. They could be the thieves Spy Center warned you about. You move past them quickly. Soon you find the maintenance tunnel.

Turn to page 12.

You pull the tunnel grate open and go inside. A few hundred feet into the tunnel, someone steps out of the shadows.

"Greetings," he says. "I am agent Rolo." He holds up two plastic chips. "We don't have much time, but I must be certain that you are really the Spy assigned to this mission. Take the chip that has the Interplanetary Spy badge printed on it."

**This one?
Turn to page 14.**

**This one?
Turn to page 34.**

If you're not sure, check the back cover of this book.

You pressed the wrong button! The platform rises up into the air, but it zigzags crazily between the tall buildings of the spaceport.

13

Finally, the platform zags when it should have zigged. This mission is over!

The End

You picked the chip with the wrong belt buckle! Rolo pulls a blaster out from under his cloak.

Without warning, he shoves you into an opening in the tunnel wall!

You slide down a long slippery chute. Finally, you land in a dark chamber. The only light in here comes from hundreds of eyes and thousands of teeth!

The End

You assemble the mask correctly, and it fits you perfectly! You take your map of Centar with you as you step out of the pod.

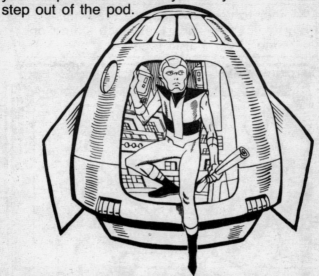

Before you enter the city you have to vaporize the pod, to make sure that no one can follow you. If you're not careful, you could lead someone to Tro—and the Star Crystal!

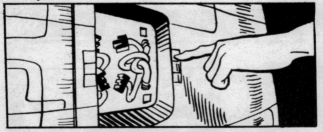

You open a box on the outside of the pod. Inside are the vaporizer controls.

Turn to page 16.

In order to vaporize the pod, you must join two cables—one from each side. Connect the plugs that fit together.

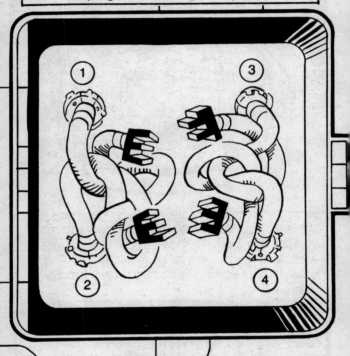

Be careful! The other two plugs are for emergency use. They should be joined only if you are about to be captured by enemy agents.

Connect 2 and 3? Turn to page 25.
Connect 1 and 4? Turn to page 20.

Inside the tower is an Interplanetary Spy shuttle craft. The shuttle will take you to the Mobius Express.

On the console you see a small opening that matches the shape of your code chip. You place the code chip in the opening. The shuttle's engines and console are activated.

Turn to page 18.

(18) Now you must set the course for the Mobius Express. On the shuttle's screen, you see the Interplanetary Spy badge magnified hundreds of times. On the badge are secret instructions written in special symbols.

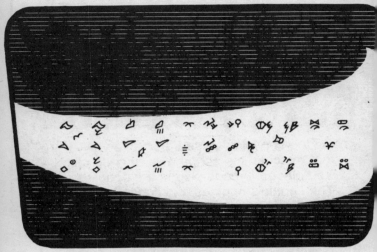

You must use straight lines to connect each symbol on the screen with the symbol that looks exactly like it. When you have done this, you will see a course number. Enter this course number into the shuttle's course computer.

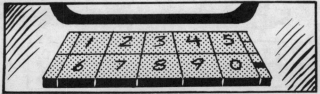

881470? Turn to page 45.

331908? Turn to page 38.

You head into the city. After a few minutes you realize that you're being followed. A gang of thieves is after you! You run into a pyramid-shaped building to get away from them.

There are two corridors in the pyramid. Which way do you go to escape the thieves?

To the left? Turn to page 30.
To the right? Turn to page 5.

If you're not sure, find the triangular pyramid on the map of Centar (see page 26). Then decide which way to go.

You have chosen the wrong cables. When they touch, the pod blows up.

Teledarian police show up to see what happened. You have nothing to show them, because the pod went all to pieces!

The End

You press the correct button, and the platform rises. The attackers may have been part of a plot to steal the Star Crystal, or they may have been a gang of Teledarian thieves. There's no way to find out now.

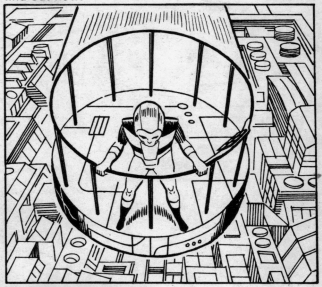

You land next to an open doorway at the top floor of the tallest building on Teledar. You enter a large apartment.

Turn to page 22.

Quarboss Tro is waiting for you. You introduce yourself as Darkstar from Interplanetary Spy Center. "Show me your code chip," he says.

You show him the chip. He nods and says, "Greetings, Darkstar. But where is agent Rolo? I thought he would be with you."

You tell Tro that Rolo was wounded as you boarded the platform. "I hope he's all right," says Tro. "But I'm glad to see that you got here safely. Now come with me. I want to show you something."

Go on to the next page.

You follow Tro to another room. The room glows with a strange and beautiful light.

"This is the Star Crystal," says Tro. "There is nothing else like it in the galaxy. That glow you see comes from deep inside the crystal. They say that it is the captured light of a dying star.

"There are beings in this galaxy that would stop at nothing to own it," says Tro, as he stares at the Star Crystal. Then, after a few moments, he says, "Let us be on our way!"

Turn to page 6.

You decide that the exploded metrobot was a maintenance type. You quickly put the pieces back together.

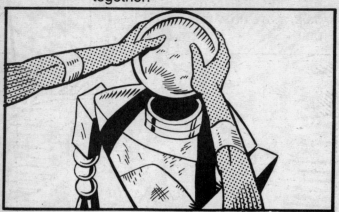

It comes to life, but something's wrong—it must have been a security metrobot.
You crossed the wrong wires. And whatever you've created is about to cross a couple of your wires!

The End

You slide the cable ends together and step away from the pod.

It works! Within seconds the pod is vaporized. You enter the city.

Turn to page 26.

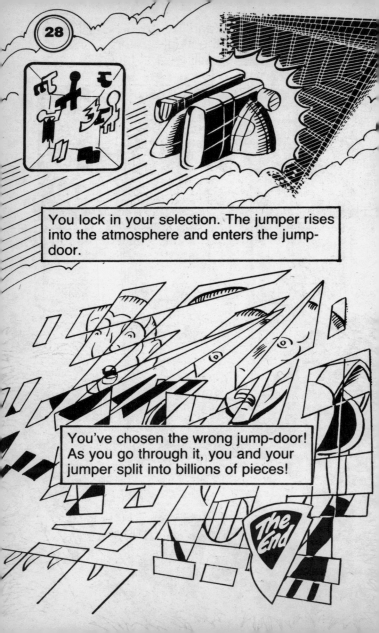

You lock in your selection. The jumper rises into the atmosphere and enters the jump-door.

You've chosen the wrong jump-door! As you go through it, you and your jumper split into billions of pieces!

The End

Heading east, you and Tro push your way through the jungle. After several hours, you still haven't found the tower. . . .

. . . But something has found you! It's hard to say what it is, but it's easy to see that it's hungry. Very hungry!

You run down the corridor to the left. At the end, you find another door. You push it open.

You went the wrong way! The thieves are outside waiting for you.

"First your money," one of them says. "And then your life!"

The End

You press the tumblers that have twelve black shapes inside. It works! The door springs open, and you enter Tro's cabin.

Quarboss Tro's lifeless body lies on the floor—and the Star Crystal is gone!

You tried to protect Tro and the Star Crystal. But still, someone got through — and it seems that Tro has paid with his life! **Turn to page 32.**

The door to the corridor is unlocked. You check up and down the corridor, but it's empty.

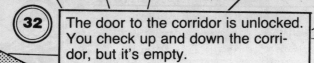

You'd like to inform Spy Center that you've run into trouble, but while the ship is in warp drive, interplanetary communications will not work. And whoever committed the crime cannot leave the ship while it is in warp drive. You must try to track down the murderer before you get to Mirado.

You search Tro's room for clues. On the floor near Tro you find a few long hairs. Which passenger had hair like these?

Check pages 66 and 67 if you need help. Then turn to page 41 when you think you've figured it out.

Your jumper rises into the atmosphere and enters the correct jump-door.

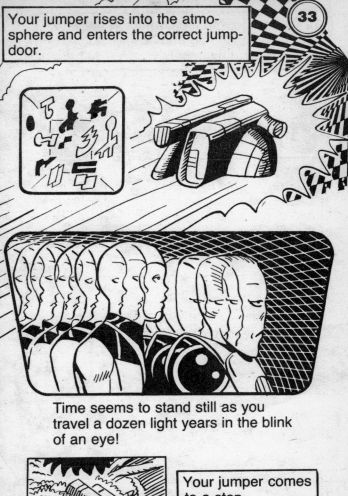

Time seems to stand still as you travel a dozen light years in the blink of an eye!

Your jumper comes to a stop.

Turn to page 42.

34

"Good. You have picked the correct chip. You are Darkstar," says Rolo. Save the chip. You will need it later to get to the Mobius Express.

"Follow me," says Rolo. "Tro is waiting in a secret apartment high above the city."

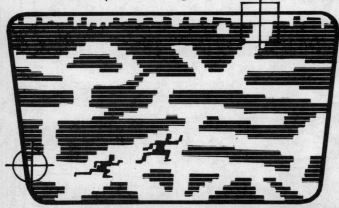

You follow Rolo through a series of winding tunnels. Finally you climb a ladder to the street above. **Go on to the next page.**

You have come up in the new section of Centar—
the spaceport. ''In the atmosphere above the
spaceport,'' says Rolo, ''there are holes in space
known as jump-doors. When a spacecraft goes
through a jump-door, it can travel through space to
distant planets.''

As you follow Rolo to a small transport
platform, you feel uneasy. **Turn to page 36.**

"We're being followed!" Rolo says. "Quick! Get onto this platform. I'll program it to take you to Tro!"

Rolo punches a series of buttons on the platform's console. "I'll stay behind to see that you get away," he says. "When you get to Grell, find the tower. Then use your code chip!" **Go on to the next page.**

Just as he's about to press the final launch button, Rolo is grazed by a blaster shot! He falls from the platform. "Get moving!" he says. "I'll be all right!"

You study the console. The buttons Rolo pressed are lit up. He pressed them following a certain pattern. You must figure out what the pattern was. Then press the tenth button to launch the platform.

ON 1	ON 2	ON 3	ON 4				
ON 5	ON 6	ON 7				ON 8	ON 9

This button?
Turn to page 21.

This button?
Turn to page 13.

331908

Good work! You enter course number 331908. The tower's roof opens and your shuttle speeds into the upper atmosphere. Within minutes you sight the Mobius Express.

As you prepare to land your shuttle on the huge spacecraft, one of its robot crew members, a metrobot, appears on your screen.

"Stand by to receive landing instructions," it says.

Turn to page 40.

"I am transmitting a diagram of the Mobius Express," says the metrobot. "You will land your shuttle on one of the two platforms. The platforms rest on conveyor belts that will move your shuttle around the ship to the passenger areas.

"Your rooms are located in the first-class section of the ship. Land your shuttle on the platform that will take you to that section." Which platform will take you to the first-class section?

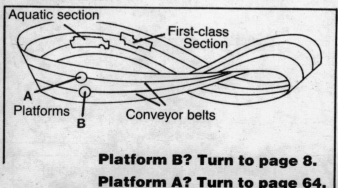

Aquatic section

First-class Section

A

Platforms

B

Conveyor belts

Platform B? Turn to page 8.

Platform A? Turn to page 64.

Callisto's pet, Tunk, has hairs like this! But that may not mean anything—the hairs may have gotten on Tro in the lounge area.

Suddenly an alarm rings in the corridor. You decide to investigate. You leave, locking Tro's cabin door behind you.

You follow a metrobot that's racing toward the alarm. **Turn to page 46.**

42 You and Tro have landed on the jungle world of sector 12. You can see nothing but the thick plant life surrounding your jumper. "I don't feel safe here," says Tro. You agree with him. There are too many places for an attacker to hide.

You decide to climb a tree so you can look for the tower Rolo told you about. "Stay close to the jumper," you say to Tro as you climb. "Call me if you need help."

Go on to the next page.

From the treetop you look out across the jungle. The sun is just rising in the east—it's still too dark to see anything clearly. You tell Tro that you must wait in the tree until the sun is fully up.

To see what the jungle looks like after the sun has risen, fold the corner of this page from point A to point B. Then find the tower.

B

Is it toward the east?
Turn to page 29.

Is it toward the north?
Turn to page 44.

You and Tro set out to the north. You push your way through the jungle plant life.

You reach the tower! It's been well hidden by Spy Center agents. "It's hard to imagine that anyone could have followed us here," says Tro.

You agree with him as you enter the tower.
Turn to page 17.

You enter course number 881470. The roof opens and you soar into the atmosphere.

In a short time, you realize that you're heading straight for the sun!

It's hot. It's very hot. It's getting hotter....

The End

As you turn a corner you see why the alarm sounded—a metrobot has been attacked!

You duck for cover as the damaged metrobot explodes!

Go on to the next page.

"This has never happened before," says a helper metrobot surveying the wreckage. Could this be connected to Tro's murder?

You decide to put the metrobot together so you can question it. "What kind of metrobot was it?" you ask the helper.

"I'm sorry," it replies. "All I can say is that according to my scan, it is not a helper type like myself."

Which metrobot type do you use as a guide in putting the pieces back together?

Security type? Turn to page 87.
Maintenance type? Turn to page 24.
If you're not sure, check page 64.

You saw that the first and third pictures feature identical drawings of flowers and were therefore by the same artist.

"Mitoshi was a great artist," says Freeba, "and you seem to be a true art expert after all. You should know, then, that my work is the best in the galaxy!

"I have the best chance of winning the Star Crystal, so why would I steal it? Please leave me alone."

You leave Freeba. You decide to speak to Callisto next. On the way to Callisto's cabin you think about Freeba. He denies the crime, even though no one said he did it. Maybe he's the guilty one!

Go on to the next page.

Callisto looks up at you as you enter his cabin.

"What do you want?" he says. "I'm busy." You tell him that you've come to visit him to see how he works.

"I work with a warp chisel," he says. "I use it to create 'impossible' shapes, like these. But you are an art expert. You should know that." **Turn to page 50.**

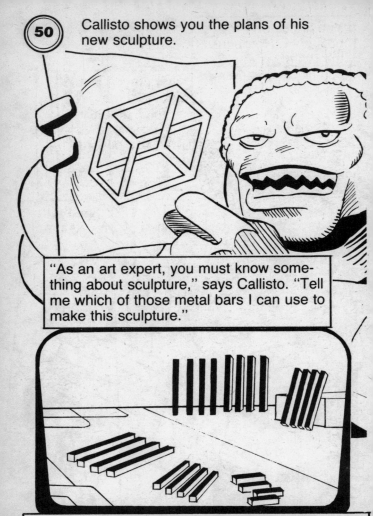

Callisto shows you the plans of his new sculpture.

"As an art expert, you must know something about sculpture," says Callisto. "Tell me which of those metal bars I can use to make this sculpture."

Do you point to the bars against the wall? Turn to page 54.

Do you point to the bars on the floor? Turn to page 59.

You knock on Free-ba's door. He opens the door by remote control, and you enter his cabin.

You tell him what happened to Tro. Freeba listens to you carefully. "I suppose that we are all suspects!" he says.

"Of course, that includes you," Freeba continues. "Maybe you did it, Darkstar! You're supposed to be an art expert, but I've never heard of you. Come closer," he says. "I want to show you something." **Turn to page 52.**

Freeba directs you to stand behind his chair. He presses several buttons on the chair's console, and four pictures appear on the chair's viewscreen.

"These are very old Japanese prints," sa[ ] Freeba. "Two of them are by one artist. [ ] other two are by two different artists."

Go on to the next pa[ ]

me, art expert," says Freeba, "which two y the same artist?"

The first and the third? Turn to page 48. The second and the fourth? Turn to page 80.

You point to the bars against the wall. Callisto, scowling, rushes over to you.

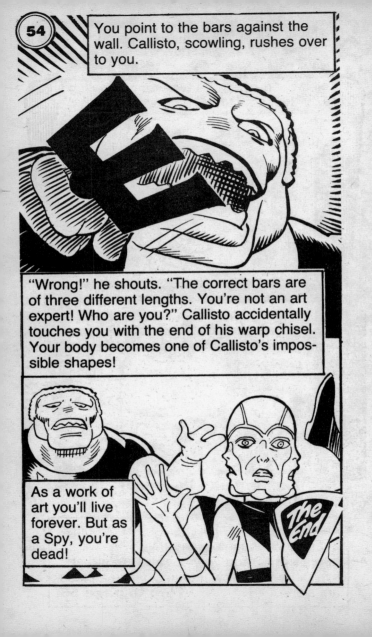

"Wrong!" he shouts. "The correct bars are of three different lengths. You're not an art expert! Who are you?" Callisto accidentally touches you with the end of his warp chisel. Your body becomes one of Callisto's impossible shapes!

As a work of art you'll live forever. But as a Spy, you're dead!

The End

The helper points to an info-screen.
"This floor plan will show you where
your cabins are located," it says.

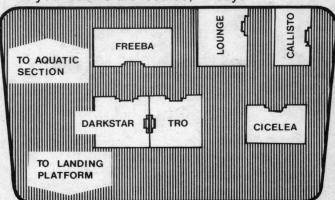

TO AQUATIC
SECTION

FREEBA

LOUNGE

CALLISTO

DARKSTAR

TRO

CICELEA

TO LANDING
PLATFORM

You see that your cabin is right next to
Tro's. "Here are your keys," says the helper. You and Tro each take two keys. One is
your cabin key, and the other is for the door
that connects the two cabins.

The helper says: "Late tonight the Mobius
Express will go into warp drive. This will
take us to Mirado very quickly. We will arrive there tomorrow morning. Have a pleas-
ant sleep." **Turn to page 56.**

You and Tro say goodnight to the other passengers. Then you see Tro safely to his cabin.

"I wish to be alone now," says Tro. "I'll leave the Star Crystal right here where I can keep an eye on it. And I'll keep the cabin door locked at all times."

"That's fine," you say, "but I suggest we leave the door between our cabins unlocked." You say goodnight to Tro and go to your own cabin.

Go on to the next page.

You decide not to sleep until you get to Mirado. After several hours, a helper metrobot appears on your cabin's viewscreen.

"Attention," it says. "We are now going into warp drive. In about three hours, we will come out of warp drive near the planet Mirado. Thank you."

A few minutes later, you hear an earsplitting scream. It's coming from Tro's cabin!

You try the connecting door, but it's been locked!

Turn to page 58.

You try your key, but it doesn't work—someone has jammed the lock!

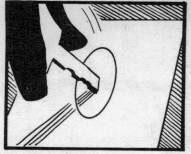

You pry the lock plate up with your key. Inside the lock box are six tumblers.
The lock is a matching tumbler system.

1

2

3

4

5

6

To open the lock, press the three tumblers that are most alike.

2-3-5? Turn to page 31.

4-6-1? Turn to page 63.

You point to the bars on the floor. "That's right," says Callisto. "To make this sculpture you need bars of three different lengths.

"But never mind this," he says. "I think I know why you're here. The news has spread.

"You're wondering if I know what happened to Tro and the Star Crystal. Well, I don't! You're wasting your time talking to me.

"If you don't believe me," he says, "go speak to Cicelea. They say she has the power to read minds!" **Turn to page 60.**

Callisto sure was eager to get rid of
What was he trying to hide? And at
same time, it almost seemed that h
trying to help you.

You arrive at Cicelea's cabin and
you knock on the door. Without saying a word, she opens the door and
waves you in.

Go on to the next pa

You ask Cicelea if she has heard about Tro. She nods her head yes and then plays her instrument—the Nautilus pipe.

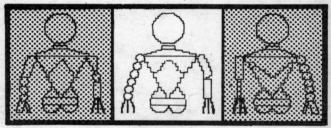

The music of the Nautilus pipe is beautiful. Its tones are like the ocean sounds you can hear when you put your ear to a seashell. You realize that this is the way Cicelea speaks—with her music alone! You call for a helper metrobot to translate her music for you. **Turn to page 76.**

You press the metrobot call button. Within seconds, the water drains out of the waterlock. The maintenance metrobot has saved you.

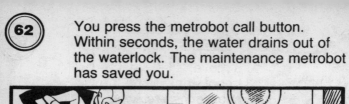

The metrobot enters the waterlock. "This room should not have filled up with water," it says, "until you put on an aquasuit.

"According to my scan, the last person to use this waterlock damaged the controls and left behind this cloak."

You've seen that cloak before, but where? **If you don't remember, check page 41. Then turn to page 68.**

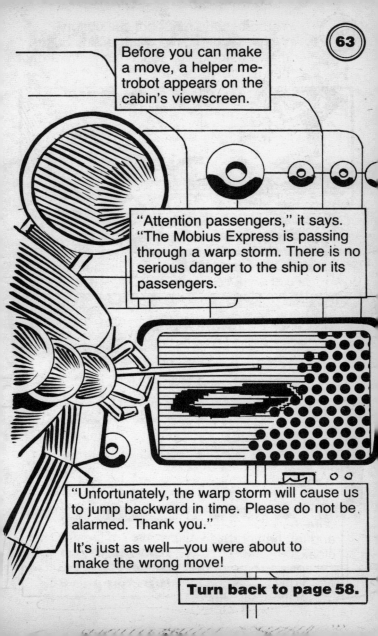

Before you can make a move, a helper metrobot appears on the cabin's viewscreen.

"Attention passengers," it says. "The Mobius Express is passing through a warp storm. There is no serious danger to the ship or its passengers.

"Unfortunately, the warp storm will cause us to jump backward in time. Please do not be alarmed. Thank you."

It's just as well—you were about to make the wrong move!

Turn back to page 58.

You land your shuttle on platform A and you begin to move toward the first-class section.

When the shuttle stops, an information chart appears on your screen. The chart shows the different types of metrobots and explains what their jobs are.

Front Views

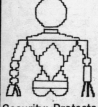

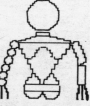

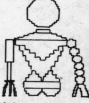

Security: Protects Ship and Passengers

Helper: Passenger Service; Translator

Maintenance: Keeps Ship Clean and in Order

Information charts like this one are located throughout the ship. From them, you can call for any type of metrobot whenever you need one. **Go on to the next page.**

You've arrived at the first-class section. Tro grips the Star Crystal case tightly as you leave the shuttle and board the Mobius Express.

A helper metrobot greets you. "Welcome aboard," it says. "Please follow me to the lounge.

"You can meet your fellow passengers there before going to your rooms for the night."

You follow the metrobot, staying close to Tro. You must be even more alert now that you are among strangers. **Turn to page 66.**

66 The helper metrobot leads you to the passenger lounge. You are introduced to the other passengers as Darkstar, an expert on galactic art.

"Darkstar is traveling with Quarboss Tro, an interplanetary diplomat," says the helper.

"The gentleman in the hoverchair is Freeba, a painter from the Ganesh Star Cluster," says the helper. "He is one of the most famous artists in the galaxy.

"Callisto is well known as a sculptor," says the helper.

"His little friend is called Tunk.

"And Cicelea is a musician and composer from the planet Ceta. She is the greatest player of the Nautilus pipe in the galaxy.

"Freeba, Callisto, and Cicelea are also traveling to Mirado. Each one has a chance to win the Star Crystal."
Turn to page 55.

As you put the aquasuit on, you realize that someone wearing the cloak passed you just before the security metrobot exploded. This cloak may be the disguise the damaged metrobot was talking about.

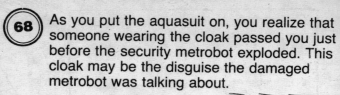

As the maintenance metrobot fixes the controls, a helper metrobot arrives. "If you wish to enter the aquatic section," it says, "you will need this package containing four ink cubes.

"When you enter the aquatic section," it says, "you will be met by the simple water creatures known as the cranex. They will guide you to their leader if you use the ink cubes correctly." **Go on to the next page.**

The metrobots leave you. Again the room begins to fill with water. "The cranex have a unique language," says the helper through a loudspeaker.

"They speak to each other by spreading different colored inks in the water around them. When you see the cranex, follow the instructions on the package."

The waterlock is now completely filled with water, and the inner door opens. You swim into the aquatic section.

Turn to page 70.

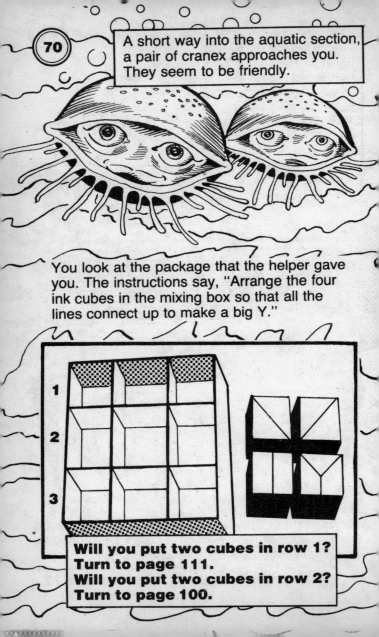

A short way into the aquatic section, a pair of cranex approaches you. They seem to be friendly.

You look at the package that the helper gave you. The instructions say, "Arrange the four ink cubes in the mixing box so that all the lines connect up to make a big Y."

1

2

3

Will you put two cubes in row 1?
Turn to page 111.
Will you put two cubes in row 2?
Turn to page 100.

You read the transla-
tion aloud: "Talk to
the water people." Ci-
celea nods again.
Then she puts the
Nautilus pipe down.
You can see that
she's now tired and
wishes to be alone.

You thank her for her help and
leave. The water people must be in
the aquatic section of the ship.

You have no way of knowing if the water people
can help you, but you're running out of time. Soon
the Mobius Express will come out of warp drive,
and the criminal will be able to escape.

Turn to page 72.

You hurry to the aquatic section—that part of the Mobius Express designed for passengers from the water worlds.

Air breathing passengers almost never visit the aquatic section. But it is possible to go there through special passageways called waterlocks.

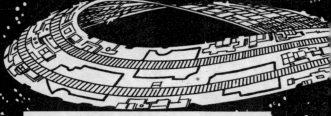

Soon you arrive at a waterlock. You can see the aquatic section through the waterlock's inner door.

Go on to the next page.

As you step inside, the outer waterlock door slams shut! Water floods the tiny room. You have to stop it before it fills completely. If you don't get help soon, you'll drown!

You check the metrobot panel—but here the panel's instructions are in a language you don't understand. You recognize the middle metrobot as a helper type, but you need a maintenance metrobot.

Do you call for the one on the left?
Turn to page 92.
Do you call for the one on the right?
Turn to page 62.
If you can't decide, check page 64.

The security metrobots aren't interested in your explanations. "Please come quietly," they say together.

The metrobots put you into a bubble cell on the surface of the ship. It's small, but it has a great view. . . . which is good, because you'll be there for a long, long time.

The End

You swim into the corridor. You go through an opening near the end, but you're not in the engineering section. You're lost!

With your mind, you try to contact Bellen, but there's no reply. You must be too far away to reach her, and you can't find your way back.

Eventually, the ship comes out of warp drive, and the criminal escapes. Enjoy your swim, Spy.

The End

The helper arrives quickly. It carries a small display screen that it uses while translating.

Cicelea plays the Nautilus pipe again. The notes she plays appear on the display, and the metrobot translates them into letters. You read what Cicelea says:

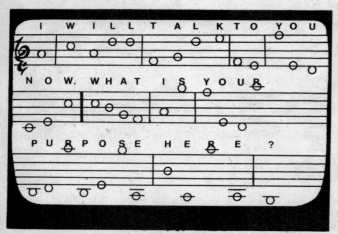

"I wish to know what happened to Tro and the Star Crystal," you say. Cicelea nods, and plays the Nautilus pipe once more.

Go on to the next page.

By comparing these notes with the ones she played before, you will be able to translate what Cicelea is saying.

Turn to page 71.

"Last night," says Tro, "I jammed the lock on the connecting door between our rooms. Then I took the parts of the fake body from a secret compartment in the Star Crystal's case.

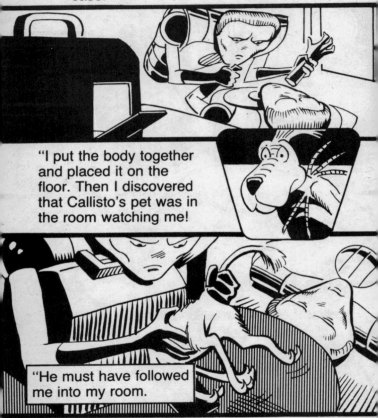

"I put the body together and placed it on the floor. Then I discovered that Callisto's pet was in the room watching me!

"He must have followed me into my room.

"I caught the animal—you probably heard him screaming. I shoved him into the Star Crystal case's secret compartment to shut him up!"

Go on to the next page.

"I put on my cloak disguise," says Tro, "and I brought the Star Crystal and the animal to my partner's cabin. I told him to get rid of the animal, but I guess he didn't complete the job.

79

"By now my partner has hidden the Star Crystal inside his artwork. We will meet on Mirado's moon, where he will give me the Star Crystal, and I will pay him for his help.

"After I left my partner, I was stopped by a security metrobot. It said that I did not look like anyone on the passenger list. The metrobot began to question me, so I destroyed it!" **Turn to page 101.**

You pick the second and fourth pictures. Freeba turns to you. "The first and third were done by the artist Mitoshi. You can tell that because both pictures contain identical drawings of flowers.

"Since you didn't know that," says Freeba, "I conclude that you are a fraud and possibly a criminal!"

Before you can say anything, Freeba presses a button, calling for metrobot security. **Turn to page 74.**

You go over to the top tube and pull the cover open. The tube seems to be empty.

You reach into the tube to see if you can feel anything inside. As you do, someone shoves you in!

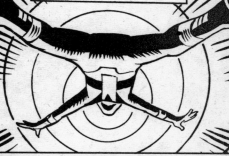

You begin the long slide to the heart of the warp engines. It seems that whoever pushed you in is getting away with two murders. Tro's—and yours!

The End

You must stall Tro until you can think of some way to escape. You say, "It looks like you have committed the perfect crime, Tro."

"Yes," says Tro, flattered by your compliment. "I think so. I have a partner, and he thinks so, too."

"You have a partner?" you ask, as you look around the room for some way to escape.

"Yes," says Tro. "One of your fellow passengers is my partner. I might as well tell you the whole story," he says, "since you won't live to repeat it!"

Turn to page 78.

It's Tro! He's alive! "I see you found the bioform body," he says. "You may have guessed that I used it to fake my own death!

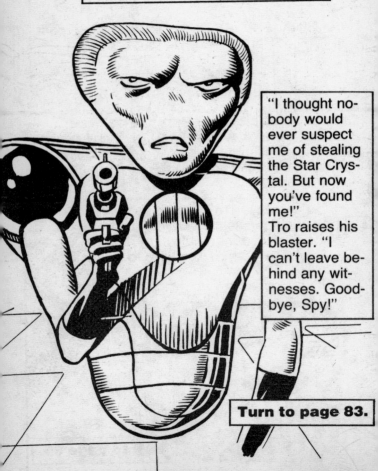

"I thought nobody would ever suspect me of stealing the Star Crystal. But now you've found me!"

Tro raises his blaster. "I can't leave behind any witnesses. Goodbye, Spy!"

Turn to page 83.

"This person," says Bellen, "went to the engineering section of the ship.

"The cranex will guide you part of the way there," she says. "Then I will telepathically show you the corridor you should follow. But remember," she says, "my eyes are on the sides of my head. I can only see to the left and right."

Turn to page 86.

The cranex lead you through a long corridor. When the corridor branches off in two directions, the cranex turn back.

Bellen telepathically sends you a picture of the corridor you must follow to get to the engineering section. But you see the corridor as Bellen sees it.

LEFT EYE

RIGHT EYE

One eye sees the left side of the corridor you should follow, and the other eye sees the right. Which way do you go?

This way?
Turn to page 75.

This way?
Turn to page 104.

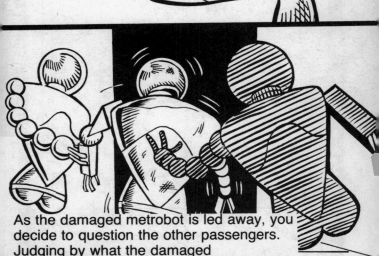

You carefully put the pieces back together. It is a security metrobot.

Soon, the security metrobot comes to life. You did well. Unfortunately, the only thing the damaged metrobot can say is. . . .

"It was a passenger . . . in disguise. . . . It was a passenger in disguise. . . . It was—"

As the damaged metrobot is led away, you decide to question the other passengers. Judging by what the damaged metrobot said, one of them may be behind the murder—and the theft! **Turn to page 88.**

You decide to speak to Freeba first, since his cabin is nearest to Tro's. You hope that he may have seen or heard something that will help you. But it is also possible that Freeba himself is involved.

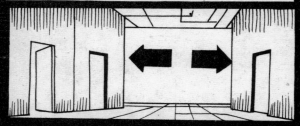

As you approach Freeba's cabin, you see that Tro's cabin door is wide open! You hurry inside.

The body is gone! It must have been taken while you were putting the metrobot together. You decide that it's time to report the crime to metrobot security.

Go on to the next page.

You call for metrobot security. When they arrive, you tell them what has happened.

"We cannot begin an investigation until we check in with headquarters. And we cannot do that until the ship comes out of warp drive," says one of the metrobots.

You know that by then it may be too late. When the ship comes out of warp drive, the criminal will be able to escape. You must track down the criminal yourself. And you'll start by talking to Freeba. **Turn to page 51.**

90

You jump to the only safe square near you as the metrobots drop to the floor. You made it!

Tro blasts the metrobot above him and heads for an open corridor. When the metrobots stop falling, you run through the corridor after him. You spot him as he gets into an emergency escape pod.

Go on to the next page.

Tro seals himself into the pod, and the launch door begins to open. When the launch door is fully open, Tro will be able to launch the pod.

If you can open the inner door, the outer door will automatically close.
That would stop Tro's escape.
The inner door is closed tightly by heavy bars. The bars are moved by gears. Which way do you turn the main gear so that the bars will move to the right and the door will open?

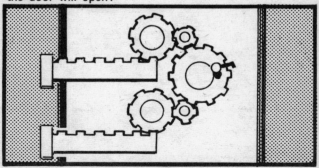

Clockwise? **Turn to page 97.**

Counterclockwise? **Turn to page 108.**

You press the metro-bot call button. With-in seconds, the water drains out of the waterlock.

As the waterlock door slowly opens, you see that you called for security metrobots! One of them drained the waterlock by remote control.

The other one says, "This waterlock has been sabotaged, and we believe that you have done it!" **Turn to page 74.**

The security metrobots take you to a shuttle capsule. It travels on the outside of the ship. As you proceed to the first-class section you say: "Callisto is your partner. The Star Crystal is inside one of his sculptures."

"How did you know that?" says Tro, astonished.

"Simple," you say. "You spoke of your partner as 'he,' so it can't be Cicelea. And it can't be Freeba, because you can't hide something inside a painting!" **Turn to page 94.**

At the first-class section you leave the capsule. The security metrobots guard Tro while you go to Callisto's cabin.

Before you can leave, Tro says: "I'm not going to rot in jail while Callisto gets away with the Star Crystal. Maybe I can help you find it!

"The Star Crystal can't be hidden in one of his warped sculptures," says Tro. "You cannot put a possible shape inside an impossible one."

You and Tro and the security metrobots enter Callisto's cabin. Cicelea and Freeba are with him. You wonder if they are in on the crime, too! **Go on to the next page.**

"Callisto," you say, "I believe that the Star Crystal is hidden inside one of your sculptures."
"Well," says Callisto, "this is a surprise. As you can see, there are only two sculptures here that could contain the Star Crystal."

Which sculpture do you think it's in?

This one? Turn to page 114.

This one? Turn to page 110.

If you don't know, check page 49.

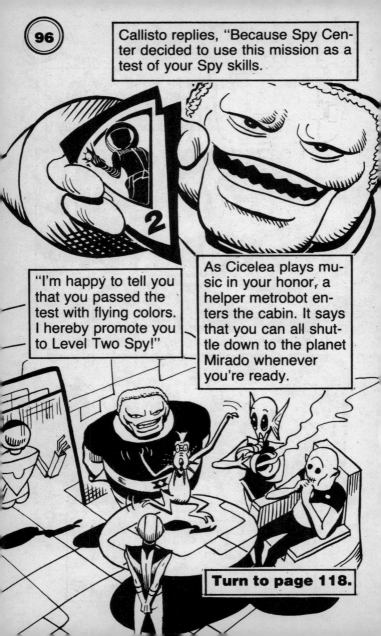

96

Callisto replies, "Because Spy Center decided to use this mission as a test of your Spy skills.

"I'm happy to tell you that you passed the test with flying colors. I hereby promote you to Level Two Spy!"

As Cicelea plays music in your honor, a helper metrobot enters the cabin. It says that you can all shuttle down to the planet Mirado whenever you're ready.

Turn to page 118.

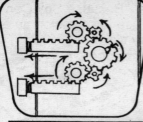

You turn the main gear clockwise. But that only seals the inner door more tightly.

The launch door opens wide, and Tro launches his pod into space! You're about to follow in another escape pod when a pair of security metrobots arrives.

"Who authorized you to use this escape pod?" they demand. You have no authorization, so you try to explain what's happened.

Turn to page 74.

You walk over to the bottom tube and pull the heavy glass cover open.

Callisto's pet leaps out, almost knocking you down! But you can see that something else is still inside the tube.

You reach in, grasp the soft, heavy object, and pull it out. **Go on to the next page.**

It's Tro! You place the lifeless body on the floor.

Tunk rushes over to you. He shakes his head back and forth and chatters. It seems that he's trying to tell you something! Could it be something about Tro's body? You study it closely.

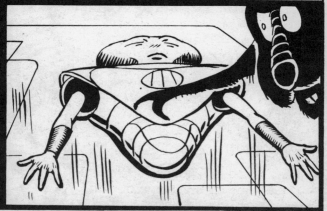

Turn to page 82.

Before Tro can finish his story, a helper metrobot appears on a nearby viewscreen. "The Mobius Express is now coming out of warp drive," it says.

You hear the sound of metal doors sliding open. "Caution in the engineering section," says the helper.

"Engineering metrobots are now being activated."
You look up. The engineering metrobots are dropping from the ceiling! **Turn to page 102.**

One metrobot is fall-
ing on Tro. Another
will crash down on
you if you don't jump
to another square
quickly.

Each metrobot will land on the square directly beneath it. You must jump to a square that will not be hit by a metrobot.

This square?
Turn to page 90.

This square?
Turn to page 121.

You swim into the corridor. At the end you go through a tunnel.

The tunnel leads to a waterlock that opens into the engineering section. You've made it! You enter the water-lock.

When the water has drained out, you find a used aquasuit. The being you're after must have left it here and must still be in the engineering section.

Go on to the next page.

You leave the waterlock and enter the engineering section.

This is where the warp engines that power the Mobius Express are located. After several minutes of searching, you hear a chattering noise, and then a loud scream!

The sounds seem to be coming from one of the reactor tubes that lead to the warp engines! **Turn to page 106.**

That same scream came from Tro's room just before the murder. The chattering sounded like Tunk, Callisto's pet.

For some reason, Tunk is in one of the reactor tubes. You can't look into the tubes because the light is too bright inside. But the thick glass cover on the end of each tube functions like a lens.

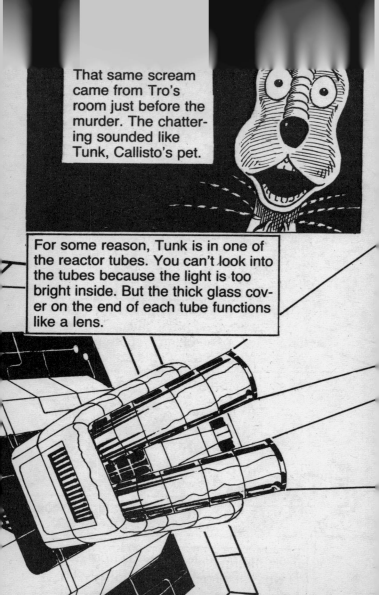

You look at the wall across from the tubes. Which of the tubes is projecting a magnified picture of part of Tunk's body?

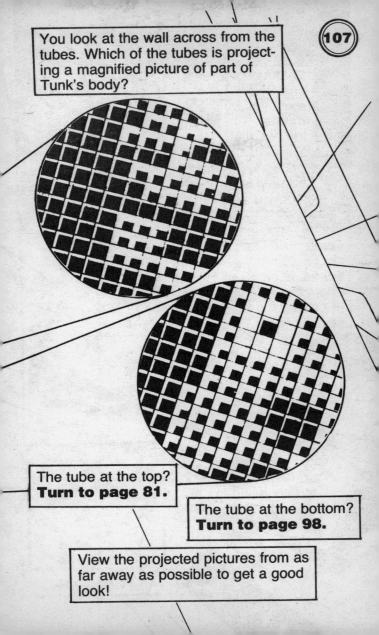

The tube at the top?
Turn to page 81.

The tube at the bottom?
Turn to page 98.

View the projected pictures from as far away as possible to get a good look!

You turn the main gear counterclockwise. The inner door opens!

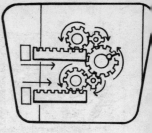

The outer launch door automatically slams shut—and the escape pod crashes into it!

You rush into the tube. Tro is dazed and confused but not too badly hurt. You pull him from the wrecked pod and take his blaster.

Go on to the next page.

"Tell me the rest of the story," you say. "All right," says Tro.

"After I destroyed the security metrobot, I passed you in the corridor. My disguise was perfect!

"But I felt there was something wrong with the fake body, so I stopped at my cabin to look at it.

"I saw that I had put the hands on incorrectly. So I took the body with me before anyone could discover it was a fake." **Turn to page 115.**

You point to the sculpture on the right. Callisto pulls the sculpture open. Inside is the glowing Star Crystal!

"You've found it!" says Callisto. "The Star Crystal is not a warped object and could not fit inside any object that was warped."

You tell Callisto that you'll take the Star Crystal to Mirado yourself. "That's fine with me," says Callisto.

Turn to page 116.

You spread the colored ink in the water around you. The cranex spread some of their own ink—it's the same color as yours. The cranex know you are friendly!

You follow the cranex through a maze of underwater corridors. You would have gotten lost in here without their help.

As you swim toward a large chamber, you hear a gentle voice in your mind. "Welcome," it says. **Turn to page 112.**

Inside the chamber is the leader of the water people. "I am Bellen," says her voice in your mind. "My people are telepathic. We speak mind to mind. So can Cicelea.

"Cicelea told me that her people were once water people. But as the water on Cicelea's world dried up, her people learned to breathe the air and live on land.

"Cicelea and her people can still speak mind to mind, but she cannot speak to beings who are not telepathic. She has asked me to help you."

Go on to the next page.

You wonder if Bellen knows anything about Tro and the Star Crystal.

"Perhaps," she says. "I told Cicelea that an air breather passed through this section several hours ago. Here is a telepathic picture as I remember it."

In your mind you see a figure in an aquasuit. It's impossible to make out who it is. But you can see that the figure is carrying Tro's body! **Turn to page 85.**

You point to the triangular sculpture. Callisto chuckles. "Sorry, Spy," he says as he pulls the empty sculpture apart. "There's nothing here."

Callisto reaches into his pocket. Is he going to pull out a weapon and attack you? Will Freeba and Cicelea help him?

Instead, Callisto shows you a Spy Center identification card! Callisto is really a fellow Spy!

"This mission has been a test of your Spy skills," says Callisto. "You did well, but not well enough to pass the test. Better luck next time, Spy!"

The End

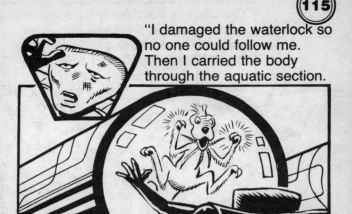

"I damaged the waterlock so no one could follow me. Then I carried the body through the aquatic section.

"While I was hiding the body in a reactor tube, I found that the animal had again followed me—probably through a small air duct. Again I managed to catch him. I threw him in the tube, too."

As you lift Tro up from the floor, a pair of security metrobots arrive to see what caused the crash. You tell them the whole story. They arrest Quarboss Tro. "Take us back to the first-class section," you say. **Turn to page 93.**

Callisto reaches into his pocket. You ready yourself. Could he be pulling a weapon to attack you with?

Instead of a weapon, Callisto shows you his Spy Center identification card! Not only is he a great artist, he's a fellow Spy as well.

"At the awards ceremony last year," says Callisto, "Tro asked me to help him steal the Star Crystal. Spy Center told me to play along so we could catch him red-handed. Cicelea and Freeba are not Spies, but they agreed to help us!"

Go on to the next page.

"Tro doesn't know it," says Callisto, "but this is special agent Tunk. He's been following Tro for almost a year!" Tro shouts, "That animal is a Spy?!"

Callisto translates Tunk's reply. "Just because you don't understand my language," says Tunk, "don't think that I'm not intelligent. A diplomat like you should know that!"

As everyone laughs in agreement, you ask, "Why didn't you tell me that all along the Star Crystal was safe?"

Turn to page 96.

Make your own Mobius Express.

1) Cut out the three pieces of the ship labeled 1, 2, and 3. You may fold them back and forth along the dotted lines, then carefully tear them from the page. You should now have three separate strips.

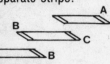

2) Using adhesive tape or glue, attach tab "B" on strip 3 to tab "B" on strip 2. The tabs should face each other directly when they are attached.

3) Attach tab "C" on strip 2 to tab "C" on strip 1. Again, the tabs should face each other directly when the strips are attached. You now have one long strip.

Turn to page 120.

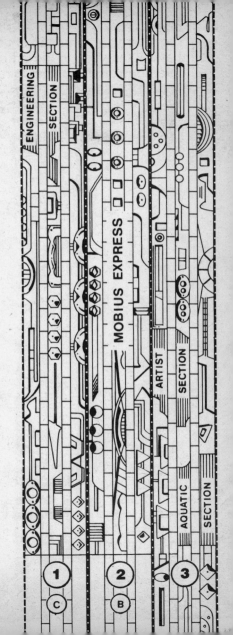

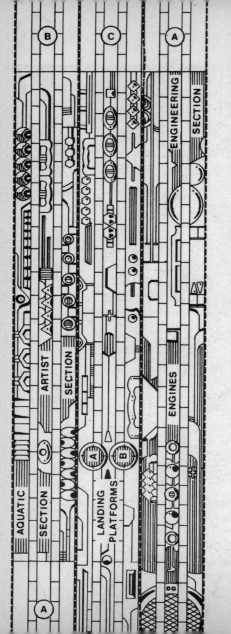

AQUATIC
SECTION

ARTIST
SECTION

LANDING
PLATFORMS

ENGINES

ENGINEERING
SECTION

A

B

C

A

4) Curl the long strip around as shown in the diagram. Both "A" tabs will be facing up, as shown.

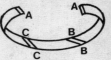

5) Twist strip 1 a half turn so that its tab "A" is facing the "A" tab on strip 3. Attach the tabs.

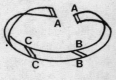

You now have a model of the Mobius Express.

If you enjoyed this book, you can look forward to these other **Be An Interplanetary Spy** books:

#1 FIND THE KIRILLIAN! by McEvoy, Hempel and Wheatley

The ruthless interplanetary criminal Phatax has kidnapped Prince Quizon of Alvare, guardian of the Royal Jewels. You must journey to the planet Threefax, find the Prince and capture Phatax!

#2 THE GALACTIC PIRATE by McEvoy, Hempel and Wheatley

Marko Khen, the Galactic Pirate, has been using his band of criminals to kidnap rare animals from the Interplanetary Zoo. You must find Marko Khen and prevent him from changing the animals into monsters.

#3 ROBOT WORLD by McEvoy, Hempel and Wheatley

Dr. Cyberg, the computer genius, has designed a planet of robots to help humanity. But the robots rebel and Dr. Cyberg disappears! You must track down Dr. Cyberg and face one of the most incredible starships in the galaxy!

#4 SPACE OLYMPICS by Martinez, Pierard and Sutton

The insidious Gresh, master spy, has threatened to sabotage the galaxy's most famous sports event. You must protect the star of the planet Nez, the superathlete Andromeda, as she makes her way through the games of the Space Olympics!

#5 MONSTERS OF DOORNA by McEvoy, Hempel and Wheatley

A mysterious tower on the planet Doorna has been sending information to Spy Center for years. Suddenly, the information stops! You must travel to Doorna and face the monsters that have been taking over the planet.